D0975569

THE CREEPER DIARIES

DIARIES

BOOK NINE

FIELD TRIP TO THE TAIGA

Also by Greyson Mann

The Creeper Diaries

Secrets of an Overworld Survivor

THE CREEPER DIARIES

BOOK NINE

FIELD TRIP TO THE TAIGA

GREYSON MANN
ILLUSTRATED BY AMANDA BRACK

Sky Pony Press
New York

THE CREEPER DIARIES: FIELD TRIP TO THE TAIGA.
Copyright © 2019 by Hollan Publishing, Inc.

Minecraft® is a registered trademark of Notch Development AB.
The Minecraft game is copyright © Mojang AB.

Sky Pony Press books may be purchased in bulk at special discounts for
sales promotion, corporate gifts, fund-raising, or educational purposes.
Special editions can also be created to specifications. For details, contact
the Special Sales Department, Sky Pony Press, 307 West 36th Street, 11th
Floor, New York, NY 10018 or info@skyhorsepublishing.com.

Sky Pony® is a registered trademark of Skyhorse Publishing, Inc.®,
a Delaware corporation.

Visit our website at www.skyponypress.com.

10 9 8 7 6 5 4 3 2 1

Library of Congress Cataloging-in-Publication Data is available on file.

Special thanks to Erin L. Falligant.

Cover illustration by Amanda Brack
Cover design by Brian Peterson

Hardcover ISBN: 978-1-5107-4103-4
E-book ISBN: 978-15107-4122-5

Printed in the United States of America

DAY 1: FRIDAY

Some mobs like to hop a minecart and head somewhere WARM in the middle of winter. Like my big sister, Cate. She'd be sunning herself in the Nether right now if she could—I mean, if Dad would let her.

But me? No, thanks. I'm not really a beach or dessert kind of guy. Oops, I mean I'm not a DESERT kind of guy. I'm definitely a DESSERT guy. I'd eat Mom's burnt apple crisp every night of the week if I could. But I'm for sure NOT a sand, camel, or cactus kind of guy. I went to the desert once for a family vacation, and let's just say that didn't go so well for me.

Anyway, when our science teacher Mr. Carl said we could SKIP SCHOOL for two weeks and take a "scientific" field trip to the Cold Taiga, I was like, "Um, WHAT now???"

Two weeks in the snowy Taiga? Two weeks of skipping school and sipping hot cocoa? Two weeks

2

of building igloos and snow golems? Two weeks of SLEDDING? Seriously??? I thought I'd died and gone to creeper heaven.

I practically flattened every other mob on my way to the sign-up sheet. I mean, here in the plains, we get snow like once a year. I wasn't going to miss out on TWO WEEKS of winter. NO way.

But I had one teensy problem. Mom wasn't crazy about the idea of the field trip. She said there weren't enough wool sweaters in the Overworld to keep me and my twin sister, Chloe, warm in the Taiga this time of year. And Mom should know—she made like a gazillion of them when she was on her knitting kick last year.

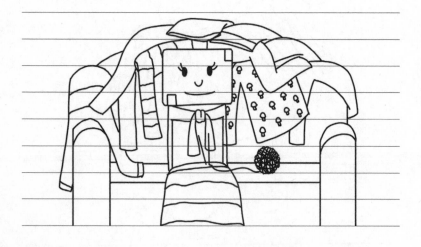

But Dad had a little talk with her. (Sometimes the old guy really comes through for me.) He said, "Honey, Mr. Carl will take good care of the kids. Besides, this will be the PERFECT way to use your new tablet. You can post messages to Gerald and Chloe on the field-trip blog!"

Well, Mom's not big on technology, so she's not exactly a whiz with that tablet. But then my big sister, Cate, showed her all the ways she could stay in touch with us, like by posting photos on Instagolem or videos on Snapghast. She could write 140-character hisses on Hisser, or create an account on Faceblock, or . . . the list went on and ON.

Well, I owed Cate BIG for that one. I mean, I was pretty sure Mom was never going to use those apps. She's not really a social media kind of mom, thank Golem. Plus, I also happen to know that kids my age aren't supposed to use any of those apps—well, except for Snapghast Kids.

But I figured it was the PERFECT time to ask Mom and Dad for a phone. All the mobs my age have them—except me and Chloe. Even Ziggy Zombie has his own phone!

His screen is crusty and disgusting, but still . . . So I asked Mom how she planned to stay in touch with me and Chloe if we didn't have our own phones in the Taiga. Genius, right?

Mom thought about it hard. I could almost hear her brain hissing. And then she and Dad had a long talk about it—a long QUIET talk. I couldn't make out a single word of it, no matter how many times I crept past the living room.

And finally, FINALLY, Mom said yes to the field trip—and yes to the phone. But only to ONE phone that Chloe and I could share. GREAT.

Chloe shares about as well as my baby sister, Cammy. If you so much as sneak a crispy potato off her plate, the little creep blows sky-high.

So I already knew Chloe was going to hog that phone—especially when Cate pointed out that Snapghast was having a *photo* contest for school-aged mobs.

I guess if you *post* a *photo* every day in March AND post the most creative photos, you can win. And Chloe? Well, she never passes up a chance to beat other mobs in ANYTHING.

I didn't care so much about the contest myself. Not at first. But get this: I found out that the winner of the contest gets (drumroll here . . .) a brand-new phone! And it's a WAY better phone than the one Mom and Dad are buying for me and Chloe to share. (They're kind of cheapskates when it comes to stuff like that.)

So now it's game on. Chloe wants to win the contest, but I'M really the creative creeper in the family. I'm always drawing and writing rap songs, so I'll probably be pretty good at taking photos too—I mean, if I can ever pry the phone away from Chloe.

If I can't, I have a backup plan. My buddy Sam will let me use his tablet. It's not great for taking photos because it's pretty much as big as my head and hard to hold on to. But hey, if it helps me win the contest, I'm all over that tablet.

So right now, as we speak, I am flying along in a minecart with Sam, heading toward the Taiga for FIFTEEN DAYS of fun and *photo* taking. (If my writing gets sloppy, DON'T JUDGE. The track is really bumpy.)

It takes TWO days just to get to the Taiga. And I can hardly wait to get out of this cart. I mean, I love Sam and all, but the slime has a way of taking over a space. He's spilling out EVERYWHERE.

Plus, he's already chatting with his cat Moo on his tablet—or at least trying to.

One of Sam's little brothers is chasing Moo around with a phone, but Moo doesn't seem all that interested in "chatting." Every time I look at Sam's tablet, all I see is cat butt.

GROSS.

I guess I should be glad Sam decided to sit with me instead of with his girlfriend, Willow Witch. Mr. Carl said we all had to buddy up, that his number-one rule on this field trip was to "stay with the group or a buddy at ALL times." That's fine by me. If I stick close to my buddy Sam, I can grab his tablet at the first sign of an award-winning *photo opportunity!*

Ms. Wanda, our other chaperone, added a rule too: that we had to learn at least ONE new thing every single day. She actually wants us to write down what we learn—to keep a list. But who'll have time for LEARNING and making lists when we're so busy DOING things?

So I've decided that I'm not going to let any rules get me down. I'm going to have fun. I'm going to have adventures! And I'm going to record it ALL on Snapghast.

The only problem? My Evil Twin keeps trying to psych me out about the wild critters in the Taiga, just like she did on our family road trip last summer. She's using OUR phone to send messages to me on Sam's tablet.

DING!

DING!

"I heard that packs of vicious wolves run WILD in the Taiga! Just sayin'..."

DING!

"You mobs better build a decent igloo—you know, to keep out the POLAR BEARS."

I pretty much never let my Evil Twin see me sweat. But she's CRAZY good at planting seeds in my head (like the way Mom plops seeds into the garden and sprinkles them with bone meal to make sure they grow). One minute, I'm not thinking about anything. Then Chloe says something, and it starts to GROW in my mind. And suddenly it's the ONLY thing I can think about!

I mean, I don't think killer rabbits are real. That's just Chloe blowing smoke. And wolves? My buddy Eddy Enderman has a wolf named Pearl, and I've hung out with her a few times. We're not exactly pals, but I don't think she'd rip me to shreds either.

But polar bears? They're a WHOLE other story.

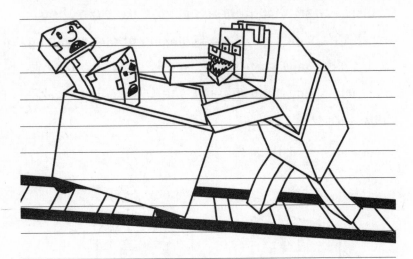

Sam saw Chloe's message and got all excited about the polar bears. "Maybe we'll see bear cubs!" His eyes got all gooey, like they do when he's loving up his cat Moo. But Sam is NOT thinking this one through.

See, I read somewhere that if you get too close to polar bear cubs, the Mom and Dad polar bears turn on you. And ALL their polar bear friends do too, like a pack of zombie pigmen. Well it just so happens that I, Gerald Creeper Jr., was CHASED by a pack of zombie pigmen during the Overworld Games last year. And just thinking about that day makes me want to hurl.

Wait. I think I'm ACTUALLY going to be sick.

Yup. Definitely going to be sick.

BLECH.

Sorry about that. I get cart sick whenever I take long rides in minecarts. The good news is, Sam just slid WAY over in the seat to give me more room—and he stopped blabbing about polar bear cubs. But I'm going to have to stop journaling pretty soon and focus on the tracks ahead. (Mom says that's supposed to make me feel better.)

DING!

Speaking of Mom, Sam says she just posted a photo of me online. "You're wearing your mushroom sweater!" he said, all happy like.

GREAT. Thanks, Mom. Thanks a lot.

Mom knit that sweater for me last year when I was going on a field trip to Mushroom Island. She COVERED it in mushrooms. Well, I'd rather freeze to death in the Taiga before letting anyone see me in THAT sweater. But now, thanks to Mom, EVERY mob in the Overworld already has.

If she'd posted it on Snapghast, it would have disappeared by now, quick as a ghast in the Nether. But she didn't. She'd posted it on the field-trip blog, where EVERY kid in these minecarts—and a couple of grown-ups too—would be sure to see it. She even added a message: "I hope my boy Gerald is wearing his favorite sweater. Stay warm, sweetie!"

PERFECT.

Mobs are snickering in the carts behind me.

"Stay warm, sweetie!" That was Bones, the most annoying spider jockey in the Overworld. I think he just flicked something at the back of my head, but I am NOT going to turn around.

I'm not going to let ANYTHING stand in the way
of me having fun on this field trip. Not Bones.
Not Chloe. Not polar bears. Not Mr. Carl's or Ms.
Wanda's rules. Not Mom's embarrassing posts. Oh,
and DEFINITELY not cat butt.

Nope. I've got a plan. And it goes something like this:

15-Day Plan for having FUN

- Don't let Chloe get inside my head.
- Find out where polar bears live — and steer clear.
- Build a snow golem that whips snowballs at Chloe until she hands over our phone. Then...
- Take awesome pictures of the Taiga and win the Snapghast contest!!!

Wait, I just thought of one more:

- Block Mom's posts so she can't TOTALLY humiliate me.

DING!

ARGH. I can't even look. Delete! Delete!

What I learned today: Keep your eyes OFF the
screen and focused on the tracks ahead.

DAY 2: SATURDAY

GLUB-GLUB-GLUB . . .

That's the sound I woke up to last night. I hollered at Chloe to get her hands out of my squid Sticky's aquarium and to get out of my room.

Then I remembered I wasn't IN my room. I was in a minecart, cruising toward the Taiga. And it wasn't Chloe making all that noise. It was SAM.

Yawwwn

I asked him what his problem was. Did he have gas? Had he eaten a hunk of cheese? (The slime is lactose intolerant, which means he can't eat cheese. Well, he CAN, but he really shouldn't.)

And you know what he said? He said that he wasn't the one making the noise—that it was my MOM. She'd posted a video on our field-trip blog. And guess who it was for?

Yup. Me. Lucky me.

"Hi, Gerald! Sticky the Squid says hello!" She waved at me with one of his tentacles. "He crawled out of his tank and into your bed yesterday. I guess he misses cuddling with you. XXOO Mom"

There were so many things wrong with that video, I didn't even know where to start. FIRST of all, I have NEVER cuddled with my squid Sticky. SECOND, Cate really needed to teach Mom that group blogs are NOT the place to post personal videos. THIRD, had Mom forgotten that she had a daughter going to the Taiga, too? Didn't she want to post embarrassing *photos* and videos about CHLOE? Like EVER?

You know, if Chloe were paying attention to all of Mom's posts, she'd be upset about that. Because it's PROOF that Mom loves me more.

Favorite Creeper Kid

Anyway, I'm AWAKE now. I just snuck a peek behind me and caught Bones, that bully of a rattler, making fun of me. His bony friend sitting in the cart next to him started laughing so hard, I thought he was going to lose his head. I could almost picture that skull bouncing away down the tracks.

Then I saw where we were. And shivered.

See, sometime during the day while we were
sleeping, we entered the Ice Plains! They're these
frozen fields FILLED with ice spikes. Some of them
are super tall and twisty, like ice sculptures. WOAH.

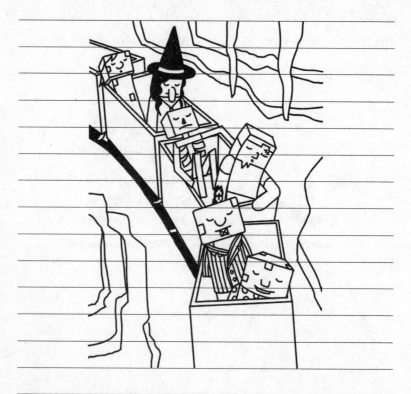

Chloe is back there using OUR phone to take
pictures. She's all about winning that Snapghast
contest. I'd fight her for the phone, but by the

time I got it, there wouldn't be an ice spike left in sight—that's just the kind of rotten luck I have.

So I reached for Sam's tablet instead. I tried to take a shot of the Ice Plains as we zoomed fast, but the tablet kind of slipped, and I got a photo of Sam's green mug. Oh, well. Not ALL my photos on Snapghast were going to be winners.

So I decided to write a rap about the ice spikes instead.

Spikes that glisten,
Yo, just listen
To the cracking ice.

Tall like towers
Feel their power
Photos would be NICE.

I know, it's not my best work, but Chloe is really getting on my nerves. I need that PHONE.

Anyway, we MUST be getting close to the Taiga now. I think I see snow falling on Ziggy Zombie's green head in the cart in front of me. (Wait, no. That's just dandruff.)

DING!

I didn't want to look, but Sam gasped, so I kind of had to. Chloe had posted a picture on Snapghast of a polar bear. An ANGRY one.

YIKES!!!

I'm not gonna lie—I practically jumped into Sam's lap when I saw that. I figured the bear was chasing the train. "Faster, Mr. Carl! Fire it up!" I might have hollered back toward the furnace cart. I could almost FEEL that bear's hot breath on my green neck!

Until Sam pointed out that the polar bear in the photo wasn't even IN the Ice Plains. He was on a snowy mountain. So Chloe had found the photo online and posted it JUST to freak me out. REALLY???

The girl had WAY too much time on her hands. So I came up with a genius idea to keep her busy. I borrowed Sam's tablet and poked out a message:

Mom. Chloe thinks you don't love her anymore. You really should start posting pictures and stuff about her online. Signed, your favorite child and Chloe's loyal and supportive brother, Gerald

SWOOSH!

That was the sound of my message flying home to Mom through cyberspace—and the sweet sound of victory. While Chloe was busy dodging Mom's posts, I'D be busy dodging snowballs and building snow golems. YAAAASSSSSSSSSS!!!

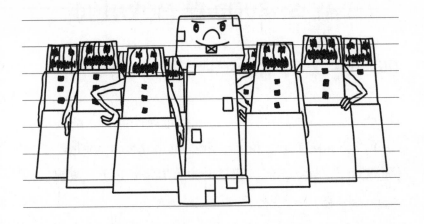

What I learned today: To keep Chloe out of my head, I have to beat her at her OWN game.

DAY 3: SUNDAY MORNING

TINK-TINK, RATTLE, TINK-TINK . . .

That's the sound of skeletons chattering their teeth, trying to get warm. Bones and his gang of spider jocks really weren't built for the Taiga. But I WAS!

As soon as the minecart stopped moving this morning, I jumped out to find the best photo ops.

But I couldn't even decide where to START. On one side of the wooden cabins was this super thick forest of spruce trees. On the other was a frozen pond.

I picked the trees, because it had been a LONG time since our last bathroom break—and because I figured polar bears hung out near water more than they did in the woods. But Mr. Carl stopped me in my tracks. "Stay with a buddy, Gerald! That's our number-one rule!"

RIGHT. I didn't love the idea of dragging Sam into the woods with me, but at least the slime was wide enough to cover me while I did my thing. And he had his tablet with him, in case we spotted something awesome in the woods. Plus, if we ran smack into a polar bear, it would probably sniff out Sam first. (I mean, the slime looks like a ginormous green fish.)

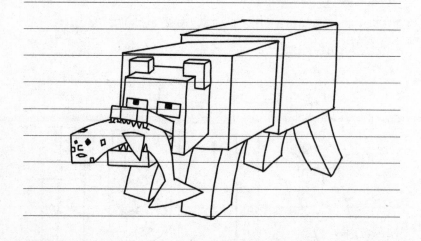

Anyway, we made it out of the woods alive. But when Mr. Carl showed us to our cabin, I found out we were bunking with Ziggy Zombie. UGH. Don't get me wrong: Ziggy and I are kind of friends. But

that doesn't mean I want to LIVE with him. He's not
exactly the cleanest mob in the Overworld.

But I forgot all about Ziggy when I stepped into our
cabin. It was just as cold INSIDE the cabin as it was
outside. We had a furnace, but there was no wood
or coal in it. HUH?

Mr. Carl said not to worry about it—that we were
going to do a little scientific experiment. "Let's
hunt for some fuel, and find out what makes the

BEST fuel for a fire in the Taiga," he said, all excited-like.

I groaned—I couldn't help it. What kind of a teacher makes his students look for their own FUEL in the Cold Taiga? SHEESH.

But finding fuel turned out to be a blast. Who knew? Ziggy, Sam, and I followed Mr. Carl's number-one rule and headed for the woods as a GROUP. We picked up big sticks right away, just in case we ran into polar bears. (And Sam seemed WAY too excited about that possibility, let me tell you . . .)

We even marked our path so we wouldn't get lost, just like Mr. Carl said we should. Well, he said we should use pieces of wood or stones to leave a trail. But we didn't need to, because Ziggy just happened to be having a snack right about then. Chunks of sandwich flew out of his mouth and landed on the ground behind him. PRESTO. That zombie is like a natural path maker. It might be his one true talent.

We hunted all over that snowy ground for wood, and we found plenty of sticks. But after a few sword fights, most of them were busted up. Then I borrowed Sam's tablet to take photos of spruce tree branches frosted with snow—THOSE were award-winning photos for sure! And THEN I got distracted by all of Mom's love messages to Chloe.

DING!

There was a *photo* of Chloe as a baby, taking a bath. "Miss my little girl!" Mom wrote. "Smooches!"

DING!

"Dad needs some gunpowder for TNT," Mom wrote. "Where's our girl Chloe with the short fuse? We miss her explosions! She's off blowing up the Taiga this week. Miss you, girl!"

Ha! I heard an explosion on the other side of the woods, which was probably Chloe blowing up when she read that message. She'd give me a turn with the phone for sure now, just to get away from Mom's posts.

DING!

Mom posted a photo of a plate of steaming-hot, burned-to-a-crisp pork chops. "Serving your favorite meal for breakfast, Chloe!" Mom said in her caption. "Yum, yum!"

Well that one really lit my fuse, because every mob knows that burnt chops are MY favorite—not Chloe's. How could Mom get that wrong??? My mouth watered the whole rest of the morning.

By the time we crept out of the woods, we only had a few measly sticks to burn in the furnace. Sam was shivering so bad, he was a jiggly green mess. But Mr. Carl took pity on us and hauled over some extra coal he had stashed in a minecart.

"He's so nice!" Sam kept blubbering. But what did he think? That Mr. Carl was going to let us FREEZE out here in the Taiga? Silly slime.

I saw Mr. Carl bring coal down to the spider jocks'
cabin, too. But in the girls' cabin, Willow, Chloe,
and her best friend, Cora Creeper, didn't need
any. Somehow, they had a fire BLAZING in their
furnace. Maybe Willow brought some potions with
her on the field trip. Or maybe Ms. Wanda was
giving the girls special treatment with a potion of
her own. No fair!

I would have raised a stink about that, but the
heat coming out of our own furnace made me so

sleepy, I could barely keep my eyes open. Sam was tired too—I could tell. He melted into a green puddle right there on the rug. And Ziggy was already fast asleep in bed, snoring and snorting up a storm.

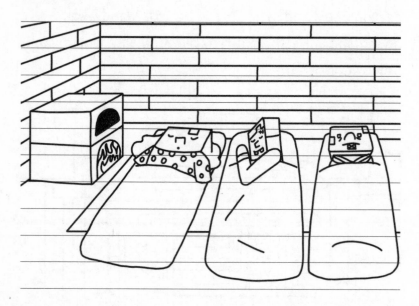

So it's time for this creeper to get his sleepers, like Dad always says.

WAIT! Crud. What did I learn today? I forgot to write it down. Ms. Wanda's rule is really messing with me.

What I learned today: Wood sticks make crummy fuel, but Mr. Carl has our back out here in the Taiga, just like Dad said he would. PHEW.

DAY 3: SUNDAY NIGHT

Okay, so I just had the WORST daymare ever.

I dreamed that our furnace ran out of coal, and I started SPOONING Sam. Like, I was so cold, I had to cuddle with that jiggly slime just to get warm.

And when I woke up tonight, I realized it wasn't a dream. And it wasn't Sam. It was ZIGGY.

Well, I flew out of our cabin like a bat out of a cave. I rolled around in the snow, trying to get rid of zombie germs. And I crossed ALL my toes, hoping that Ziggy had slept through the whole thing and wouldn't remember.

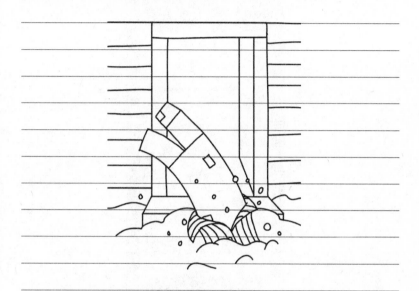

But he did. Yay. Lucky me.

"Thanks for warming me up today, Gerald!" he grunted, wiping a stringy hunk of carrot off his chin. "It was FREEZING in here!"

Aw, MAN. Mom might as well post that on our field-trip blog: "Son found spooning zombie for survival."

Then it would go viral, and I'd be the laughing stock of the whole Overworld.

Luckily, zombies aren't the brightest torches on the wall. I told Ziggy he must have been dreaming— that I hadn't even SLEPT today because I'd been so excited about igloo-building.

"Yup," I said, brushing snow off my shoulder. "I was outside all day scouting a spot for our igloo."

"Really?" said Ziggy. He forgot about the spooning incident and staggered for the door. "Show me where!"

So now I'm going to have to come up with some epic spot for igloo-building. Maybe we'll walk outside and my gut will just lead me to the perfect site. (Hey, it could happen.)

But first, my gut needs FOOD. I'll bet Mr. Carl and Ms. Wanda have something DELICIOUS cooking up for us in the main cabin. Maybe roasted pork chops and crispy little potatoes!

I'll take a _photo_ and _post_ it on Snapghast. Maybe I'll text it to Mom too, to remind her that it's MY favorite meal, not Chloe's. SHEESH.

And then? I'm hitting up Chloe for the phone. My turn is WAY overdue.

DAY 4: MONDAY

You know, I think Mr. Carl might be taking our science lessons WAY too far.

When we got to the main cabin last night, there was NOT a delicious meal waiting for us. Nope. Mr. Carl told us that the fuel we gathered yesterday wasn't just for heat. It was also to help us make food—our OWN food.

When I heard that, my stomach twisted into knots. SERIOUSLY? Couldn't Mr. Carl just skip the learning part and jump ahead to the "Ms. Wanda and I cooked this delicious meal for you as a backup" part?

The only good thing that happened in the main cabin was that Chloe gave me the phone. In fact, it seemed WAY too easy. I asked for it, and she gave it to me. HUH. THAT was a first. But when I stepped outside, I realized why. There was only one bar of service, and it kept fading in and out.

When Sam, Ziggy, and I headed back into the woods, there was NO service. I guess the trees were too dense. GREAT.

This fuel-gathering trip was WAY less fun than the first one. Ziggy didn't leave a trail of food chunks—he'd eaten all of those. And we didn't have sword fights. Nope. We were going to find every single stick in the woods, and every mushroom for mushroom stew.

But here's the thing: there aren't a lot of mushrooms growing in the snow. When I found one popping out, I tried to post a photo of it—all cute, and round in a patch of white.

But my dumb phone still had NO service.

Lucky for me, Sam's tablet DID. So he let me take a quick pic. Then I picked the mushroom. Then I popped it into my mouth.

"Hey!" he said. "We're supposed to bring them back to camp for mushroom stew!"

But I couldn't help it. Every time I found a mushroom, it leapt right into my mouth. I guess this camping in the Taiga thing was making me hungry.

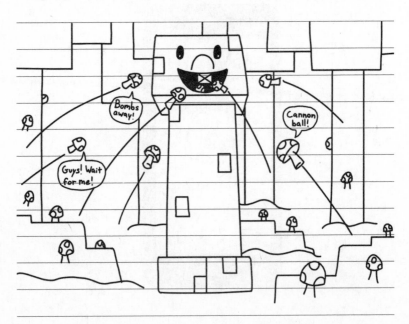

Besides, I knew Mr. Carl wouldn't let us STARVE to death out here. If we didn't have enough mushrooms for stew, he'd serve us up something else, right? So we just had to get through the stew-making lesson and on to bigger, better, and tastier things.

Like the pork chops he had frying in the main cabin for mobs who weren't able to find any mushrooms. YAAASSSSSSSS!!!!

I knew it! I knew he had our backs! A part of me wanted to point out to Mr. Carl that he wasn't really teaching us much about science. He was actually teaching us that we could just have FUN and he'd take care of everything else. But another part of me told that first part to pipe down—that I had a good thing going here and shouldn't blow it.

So I filled up on chops. When Chloe asked for our phone back, I gladly gave it to her. I mean, what good was it out here anyway?

Then I hauled a whole bunch of Mr. Carl's coal back to our furnace so we wouldn't run out again. I will NOT be spooning a zombie again any time soon. No sirree.

Later, when Mr. Carl and Ms. Wanda said we could build igloos, I nearly leapt out of my creeper skin.

FINALLY!!! We were done with lessons and were going to have some FUN.

I thought Mr. Carl would just turn us loose on the snowy mountain. WRONG. He said he wanted to teach us some "engineering basics."

SERIOUSLY??? How hard did he think it was to build an igloo? You just stack snow blocks on top of snow blocks. What did he think we were—poor mobs from the Nether who had never even SEEN snow?

Mr. Carl drew this super-complicated diagram of a curved roof. "Pay attention," he said. "You don't want your roofs caving in on you, do you?"

He kind of had a point there. So I tried to watch while he drew diagram after diagram (after diagram . . .). Then Ms. Wanda got in on the action and said we should sketch out our igloos on paper before we built them.

Next thing you know, my head was bobbing with boredom, because I felt like I was back in school—studying diagrams and making dumb drawings instead of actually DOING something. What a snooze!

Sam sketched us out a pretty decent igloo. I mean, it was more of a square than a circle. But whatevs. When Mr. Carl said it was finally time to start building, Ziggy staggered over and said, "Okay, Gerald! Show us the spot you picked out!"

UH-OH.

I had to play it cool, which isn't easy when all the other mobs seem to know JUST where they're going to build.

Bones and his buddies rattled toward the pond. Willow Witch, Chloe, and Cora crept uphill. So while Mr. Carl hissed at us to "Stay together! Stay with your groups!" I had to think fast.

Why were the girls hiking up a hill? Then it hit me—because THAT's where we'd actually have phone service.

"C'mon!" I said to Sam and Ziggy. "Time for a climb."

The girls hiked pretty high before finding a flat spot to build on. But we hiked even higher. Finally there was a flat patch of ground, but it wasn't very big.

"Is this it?" Ziggy asked, panting. He didn't look very impressed.

"Yup," I said super confident-like. "This is definitely the best spot. DEFINITELY."

So he shrugged and started packing blocks of snow.
Ziggy is a pretty easy-going mob—just like Sam.
Those boys got to work, and before I knew it, we
had a ring of snow blocks.

"It's not very wide," Sam said.

"So let's build it TALLER!" I said. But we didn't have
very much snow to work with.

Down below us, the girls were building like CRAZY.
Pack, stack, pack, stack, pack, stack. It was like
watching a video on Snapghast that was all sped up.
My Evil Twin was moving so fast, she was a green blur.

Then it hit me. They were using potion of swiftness! I'd seen Willow use it to build a snow fort last winter. I didn't mind then, because she was building the fort with me and Sam. But now?

I minded. Yeah, I minded a lot. Because the girls had a huge igloo built before we could even add on to our wall. And their igloo was BLOCKING the view from our igloo! NOT fair!

Sam reminded me to pay attention to what I was doing. I guess I got kind of sloppy with the snow blocks. "We have to curve the roof!" he said, waving his sketch in my face.

But how could I focus on our *pathetic little igloo* when the girls were adding a full CHIMNEY onto their own? SHEESH.

When they disappeared inside the igloo, I tried to peek through a window to see what was going on. That's when Willow added a pane of ice—FROSTED ice. Then I pretty much couldn't see anything.

Especially when smoke started pouring out the top of the girls' igloo. And because OUR igloo was up above theirs on the hill, the smoke was pretty much blowing right in my face.

"They built a FIRE," I said, after a huge coughing fit.

"Awesome!" said Ziggy, rubbing his hands together.

"Ours will be MORE awesome," I said.

Sam had barely finished the roof of our igloo before I lit a few sticks inside with flint and steel. He was trying to tell me something, but I couldn't really hear him over our crackling fire.

Yup, I got that baby roaring. Bust out the marshmallows and hot cocoa, because our fire was burning HOT.

I started to sweat. Then I realized it wasn't sweat—it was water dripping from the ceiling. A LOT of water. Next thing you know, our whole ROOF caved in! Right on our fire. Right on ME.

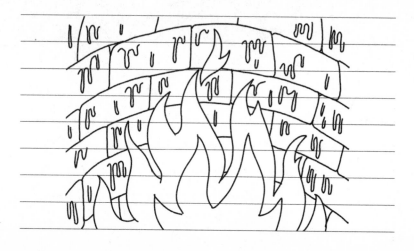

Turns out, if you're going to build a fire in an igloo, you have to leave a hole in your roof for the smoke to go through. HUH.

"I tried to tell you," Sam kept saying. He showed me the vent on his sketch, which was now soaking wet.

I wish he'd tried a little HARDER.

He and Ziggy wanted to fix the roof right away, but I said maybe we could do it later—after a good day's sleep. I mean, a roof had pretty much just crushed me. I wasn't much feeling like building another one. So we took a photo of Sam's sketch before it totally fell apart. Then we headed back down the hill toward the cabin.

Chloe had the nerve to poke her head out the front door of her igloo and brag that she and the girls were SLEEPING in their igloo today. "Who needs a cabin?" she said, all smug-like.

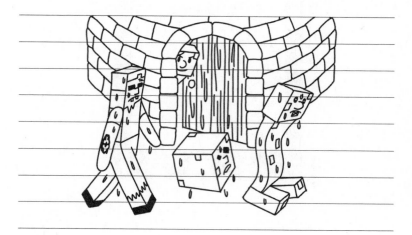

Well, first of all, who puts a wooden DOOR on an igloo? How'd the girls get that made so fast? What kind of potions was Willow brewing in there?

Chloe snapped a photo of my surprised face—with the phone she's SUPPOSED to be sharing with me—

and slammed the front door. I guess she's got service again, which means my mug will be featured on Snapghast any second now.

When we got back to our cabin, I remembered that I hadn't posted a photo to Snapghast yet today. And I'd only taken a single photo—the one of Sam's igloo sketch. So I posted that online. Why not?

Like I said, not ALL of my Snapghast photos are going to be winners. Just like not all my fifteen days here in the Taiga are going to be winners. Today was definitely NOT.

What I learned today: Where do I start? Let's see. DON'T waste time gathering food—Mr. Carl has that covered. DO spend time paying attention during igloo-building lessons. DON'T try to use a phone in the woods. DO head uphill when you want service. DON'T be surprised when Chloe cheats—especially when she's bunking with a potion-brewing witch. DO try to listen to Sam when he talks. The slime knows a thing or two about a thing or two.

Whew! That's a lot of learning for one day. Ms. Wanda would be proud.

DAY 5: TUESDAY

So when I woke up last night, Sam was gone.

Ziggy was snoring up a storm, but Sam was nowhere to be found. UH-OH. I wondered if I'd driven my buddy away with the whole "ruining the ceiling of our igloo" thing.

But when I headed outside, I heard his jolly laugh. From up on the hill. So I guess he'd decided to hang out with his girlfriend for a while in her igloo mansion.

I crept up the hill to spy on them, but like I said, those frosted windows aren't very easy to look through. And somehow, Chloe knew I was out there. She flung open the door and told me to get my sneaky creeper butt inside. I think what she REALLY wanted to do was show off her igloo.

I gotta say, it was pretty impressive. The fire pit was roaring. Willow must have used a blaze rod to light that thing or something, because it didn't look like it was going to burn out anytime soon—like ever.

Cora gave me a quick tour. There was a crafting table in the corner, which explains how they made a door. And three beds. And a torch chandelier. And a woven carpet on the floor. SHEESH.

I don't think Mr. Carl could even make an igloo like this, no matter how many diagrams he drew first. Chalk one up for potion of swiftness.

I could tell that Chloe wanted me to say something about the igloo—to pay her a compliment or something. But I couldn't cough one up. Instead, I asked for the phone back. "It's my turn," I said.

"Not yet," she said. "I need to post a Snapghast photo first."

But half an hour later, at dinner, she couldn't WAIT to give me the phone. I realized why as soon as I saw Mom's mug, larger than life, on the screen.

Mom
Calling

Accept Decline

UH-OH. I guess Cate had finally taught Mom how to video-chat. And Chloe made sure to hit the "accept" button before tossing me the phone like a hot potato. GREAT.

"Hi, honey!" Mom hollered really loud, like she didn't think I could hear her through the phone. But EVERYONE in the cabin heard her—from Ms. Wanda in the kitchen to Bones and his buddies sitting way at the back table. "How's my boy?" Mom shrieked.

I TRIED to lower the volume. But I somehow turned Mom's voice UP instead of DOWN. "Oh, I miss you so much!" she bellowed.

<u>NO!!!</u>

<u>When Mom made smoochie noises, I sprinted out of</u>
<u>the cabin and practically dove into a snowbank.</u>

I love you oodles!

<u>Remember when I said I have rotten luck? Well, last</u>
<u>night was PROOF of that. I mean, Chloe couldn't get a</u>
<u>signal down here at the bottom of the hill for DAYS.</u>
<u>But when Mom called and I had the phone, I SUDDENLY</u>
<u>had reception. Not just one or two bars, but THREE.</u>
<u>Yup. Mom was coming through LOUD and clear.</u>

"What's wrong, honey?" she kept asking. All I could see was her mouth now, like she thought if she held the phone to her lips, I'd hear her better.

"NOTHING, Mom," I said. "Except that my phone battery is going to die ANY minute now, so we'd better keep this short, okay?"

I reassured her that everything was fine. That I was wearing my sweaters. That there were no polar bears near our camp. That I was eating at least two square meals a day and obeying all of Mr. Carl's rules.

"But the phone's going to die in a few seconds, so I'd better go!" I said.

"Oh, okay, honey. Give Chloe a kiss—"

I hung up on Mom right there and then, because there would be NO kissing of my Evil Twin. Not after the stunt she'd just pulled.

I couldn't go back into the cabin for breakfast. Bones and his buddies would eat ME alive, after hearing my video-chat with Mom. So instead, I took a picture of the moon rising over the pond. Might as well post on Snapghast while I still had reception.

I even wrote a rap about it. What can I say? I guess being cold and hungry inspires me.

Then I headed back to our sleeping cabin and thought about what I'd learned.

What I learned (ALREADY) today: When Chloe is dying to give me the phone, I probably SHOULDN'T take it. I should turn around and RUN.

DAY 6: WEDNESDAY MORNING

Things started looking up last night. Why? Because Ms. Wanda said we could finally make SNOW GOLEMS!!!

I guess she'd been storing some pumpkins for us in the main cabin. They were smooth and orange and PERFECT.

Ziggy Zombie didn't think so. He's more of a fan of moldy, rotten jack-o-lanterns. But I got one of those stinky, slimy things stuck on my head once, so I can't even SEE a jack-o-lantern without wanting to hurl.

Anyway, Ms. Wanda didn't make us study a bunch of diagrams before we made our golems. She's an art teacher, so she's all about creativity. Besides, what's so hard about stacking a couple of snow blocks and sticking a pumpkin on top?

Sam wanted his snow golem to have only one snow block—so it would be square like him. But snow golems don't really work that way. I tried to tell him, but sometimes a slime has to learn things for himself.

Ziggy stuck a couple of sticks in the front of his so it would look like a zombie staggering around with its arms outstretched. WEIRD.

I kept mine simple. I only wanted one thing: a snow golem that could throw a decent snowball. So I gave mine super sturdy branches for arms.

I happen to know that snow golems are really loyal. So, like, if Bones and his gang whip a snowball at me, guess who will protect me? My golem! He'll zing snowballs right back at Bones. Or Chloe, for that matter. In fact, after she forced me to video-chat with Mom in front of EVERYONE yesterday, I'd MUCH rather zing HER with a snowball than Bones.

So as soon as I propped my pumpkin up on top of my snow golem, I couldn't WAIT to see him come to life. And he did! His pumpkin head turned just a bit so he could take a good long look at me.

That kind of creeped me out—but only for a second. Then I quickly snapped a photo of him for Snapghast. If I don't post a photo right away at night, morning comes fast—and then I'm stuck posting dumb photos like a sketch of an igloo or the side of Sam's head or even my foot (that photo was an accident, but SOMEONE out there might think it's actually art).

Anyway, my snow golem started slipping and sliding around the snowy field. Ziggy's was "alive," too, sliding toward me with its creepy zombie arms. Yikes!

Even Sam's short little golem somehow worked.
When he added a pumpkin head, the golem started
to move—but REALLY slowly.

"Huh," said Sam, his forehead all scrunched up. "Is
yours faster than mine?"

Mr. Carl heard him from way over by the cabins.
"That's a GREAT question, Sam," he said. "A
SCIENTIFIC question. Should we test it out?"

SIGH.

Now instead of just hanging out and having snowball
fights with our golems, Mr. Carl was going to turn
the whole night into a science experiment.

Next thing I knew, he had us counting the number of seconds it took for our golems to move like three feet. I didn't think that was very scientific. First of all, you can't MAKE a golem move, not like in a race anyway. And none of us had tape measures or rulers. We were just guessing how much was three feet. And to top things off, I'm PRETTY sure Willow Witch was using a potion of swiftness with her golem. That snow golem moved across the snow so fast, I thought it was a polar bear.

When I told Mr. Carl that the girls were cheating, Chloe made a face at me and whipped something at my snow golem—a glass bottle. I couldn't believe it. Chloe was throwing SPLASH potions now? (Note to self: I really have to break up her friendship with Willow Witch. It's going nowhere good.)

I didn't know what kind of potion it was until I happened to run right THROUGH it. "Gerald, stop!" Sam yelled. But it was too late. I barreled through the cloud of purple dust.

Right away, I felt like I was in a daymare, like when you're trying to run away from the Ender Dragon but your legs just won't MOVE. Everything happened in slow motion. My phone bounced on the ground and kind of floated back up again, right toward Chloe. She grabbed it, flashed her evil grin, and took off running. Score one for my Evil Twin.

My snow golem slowed way down too, almost as slow as Sam's. Good thing I wasn't measuring my golem's speed right now—he was almost moving BACKWARD, he was going so slow.

"What . . . HAP-PENED?" I asked Sam, but it took forever to get the words out of my mouth.

"Lingering potion of slowness," he said with a jiggly shrug. I guess when you date a witch, you pick up on stuff like that. But all I wanted to know was how to get the potion OFF me.

Sam read my mind. "It'll wear off pretty soon," he said, and he was nice enough to squat down beside me. But that made us sitting targets for Chloe, who took that opportunity to bean me with a snowball.

I tried to get up and tackle her, but my body was practically frozen to the ground. Then I realized something. Chloe's snowball would start the PERFECT snowball fight, because my snow golem would protect me, right? RIGHT???

WRONG. My golem slid slowly down the hill, AWAY from Chloe.

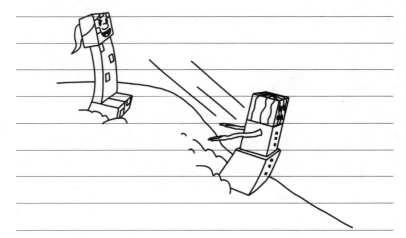

"Hey!" I hollered to Sam and Ziggy. "My golem doesn't work! It won't throw snowballs at Chloe."

"Snow golems DON'T throw snowballs at creepers, genius!" That was Bones. Then I heard the thwack

of his bow and arrow and *the smuck* of a snowball
against the back of my head. OUCH.

I was face-planted in the snow when I realized
Bones was right. I'd heard that before—that snow
golems won't throw snowballs at creepers. Why?
I dunno. Maybe we're just naturally friends or
something.

That should have made me feel all warm and fuzzy
toward my golem, but it didn't. I wanted to start
throwing snowballs at HIM for not backing me up

against Chloe. SHEESH. What does a creeper have to do to get some good help around here?!

Anyway, it turns out that snow golems DO throw snowballs against skeletons, because after Bones nailed me with the snowball, my golem came BACK up the hill—and lobbed a snowball at Bones. YAASSSSSS!

That's when a full-on war broke out.

Snowballs zinged left and right, and when the potion of slowness wore off, I could finally dodge

the balls and fling a few of my own. But Bones was WICKED with that bow and arrow. When I took a ball of ice to the nose, I tasted the blood before anyone else even saw it.

Well, I went straight to Mr. Carl with my bloody nose, because bows and arrows have NO place in snowball fights. He gave me a stained yellow handkerchief, which totally grossed me out. And to make matters worse, he DIDN'T make Bones put away his bow and arrow. Instead, he turned it into a science experiment.

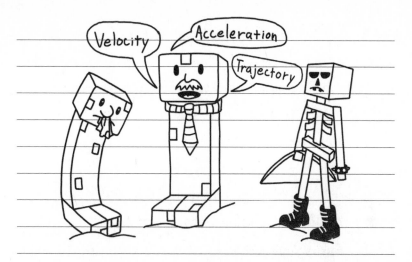

When he started to talk about the "trajectory" of Bones's snowballs off his bow, he lost me. He lost Bones, too, who rattled off toward his cabin like he was going to put his bow away before Mr. Carl started quizzing him on how it worked. So score one for Mr. Carl, too—he bored Bones into good behavior.

Mr. Carl looked kind of disappointed, until someone else asked, "How long before the snow golems melt?" Then his eyes lit up and he turned THAT into an experiment. "Let's test it out!" he said, all jolly-like.

But that's one experiment I will NOT be taking part in, thank you very much. I mean, I just GOT my golem. And maybe he's not going to take my side against my Evil Twin, but he'll be great for Snapghast photos—I mean, if I ever get my phone back from Chloe.

After a while, some of the golems wandered away. I guess that's what they do—they get bored just like we do. Ziggy's golem slid off toward the woods with its arms outstretched. Sam's took off, too, super slowly. It left a wide path of snow.

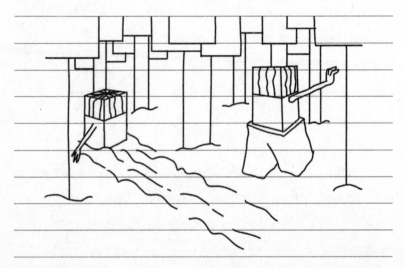

"Do you want to follow it?" I asked. "It's leaving a decent trail."

But Sam just shook his head. I think his super-wide, super-slow golem had been kind of a disappointment right from the start.

But mine? I was NOT ready to let mine go yet. So you know what I did? I brought it home with me.

Not to the cabin—it would melt for sure in there. No, I brought it to our igloo instead. See, I figured it would stay nice and cold in there, but I could block the door with a giant snowball to make sure the golem didn't wander away. I even decided to hang out in there with him so he wouldn't get lonely.

At first, my golem kind of paced back and forth inside the igloo. But then I must have fallen asleep, because next thing I knew, it was almost dawn, and the golem was GONE. The snowball had been pushed away from the door of the igloo, and my snow golem's path zigzagged across the hill, just BEGGING me to follow it.

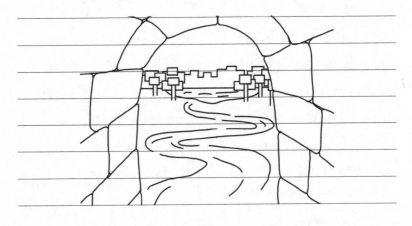

Now I know all about Mr. Carl's rules. I KNOW I'm supposed to stay with the group and not wander away without a buddy. But my snow golem IS kind of my buddy, right? He protected me against Bones, didn't he?

So before I could talk myself out of it, I followed that path, straight down the hill toward the pond.

I'm not gonna lie, I DID think about polar bears. I was the only mob out there so early in the day. If a polar bear wanted to eat me up, I'd be like the last cookie on a plate—all alone and easy to grab. CHOMP.

But I didn't see polar bears. I saw something else.

WOLVES.

Well, paw prints in the snow, anyway. They looked just like the prints Eddie Enderman's wolf-dog, Pearl, made when she pulled me in a minecart sled last winter.

Now some mobs might be scared to see those paw prints. And I did look over my shoulder, wondering if the wolves out here in the Taiga were more ferocious than Pearl.

But then I thought about something else: what an AWESOME photo I could take of these paw prints in the snow. Suddenly, I couldn't WAIT to take the photo. It would be an award-winner for sure!

I forgot all about my golem and raced back to the cabin. Sam was just getting ready for bed, and Ziggy Zombie was already out cold—like a torch someone had just put out with a bucket of water.

I asked Sam if I could borrow his tablet to take a photo. Then I had a better idea—I asked Sam to come WITH me on an adventure. I mean, if we DID run into polar bears, I'd be a lot less scared with Sam by my side. (And I'd have only half the chance of being eaten too.)

Sam said YES—that slime is game for anything. But he's been looking for his scarf for like ten minutes now, so I thought I'd catch you up on the night's events. I have a feeling that today is going to be EVEN more eventful.

Snapghast photo awards, here I come!

DAY 6: WEDNESDAY NIGHT

What I learned today: Don't post things on Snapghast that you don't want Chloe—or Mom—to see. SIGH.

Okay, let me back up. Sam went with me to get a shot of the wolf paw prints. And it was a PERFECT photo, if I do say so myself. The lighting was just right. I centered the paw prints just so. I zoomed in to make them look even BIGGER. And then right away, at 7:35 a.m., I posted it to Snapghast.

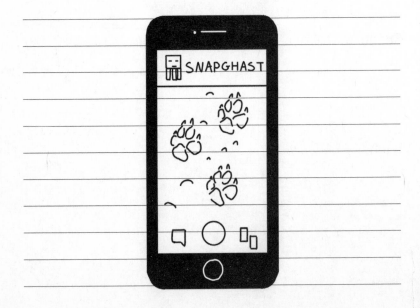

Well, Chloe must have been really impressed with that photo. How do I know? Because she texted Mom IMMEDIATELY to rat me out and try to get me in trouble.

Chloe told Mom that I broke all kinds of rules and wandered away from my cabin during the day. But I HADN'T broken any rules. I had my buddy SAM with me, for crying out loud. And my snow golem was out there too—somewhere.

Anyway, when Mom video-chatted me on Sam's tablet ten minutes later, she said she didn't care if I had a whole ARMY of snow golems with me. She did NOT want me anywhere near a pack of wolves. (Mom can be kind of dramatic when she wants to be.) "Did Mr. Carl know you were out there?" she demanded to know.

"No, he was sleeping," I said. What else could I say? I mean, if I'd lied and told Mom that Mr. Carl DID know I was out there with the wolves and all, he'd be in trouble too. Right?

Except that plan backfired.

Mom called Mr. Carl and gave him a piece of her mind. She said that chaperones weren't supposed to SLEEP on the job. She said she'd be talking to the principal of Mob Middle School about this. And then she posted a message on the blog warning ALL the other parents to stay in touch with their kids to make sure they weren't "wandering all over the Taiga in the middle of the day unsupervised."

Well, you can imagine how popular THAT post made me today. By the time all the mobs got up and headed to the main cabin for dinner, almost every single one of them had gotten a warning text from their parents. Thanks to me.

To top it off, Mr. Carl has a new rule: NO leaving the cabins after bedtime. He even threatened to lock us all in, just to be sure. Oh, and he says we won't be making any more snow golems during this field trip. And he looked right at me when he said it.

Personally, I think Mr. Carl doesn't like snow golems because he can't CONTROL them with all his rules. He can't lock them in cabins or make them learn things when all they REALLY want to do is wander around and throw a snowball or two.

If you ask me, the snow golems have the right idea. But no one did ask me. Because no one is really talking to me right now.

So like I said, when you're gonna post something to Snapghast, you really have to stop and think about WHO is going to see your post. And just how much TROUBLE it might get you into.

Photo contest or no photo contest, a creeper's really got to think ahead.

DAY 8: FRIDAY MORNING

"You skipped a day, Gerald!"

That's what you want to tell me, right? But if you knew how BORING Thursday was, you'd thank me for leaving it out of my journal.

See, Mr. Carl and Ms. Wanda decided we needed a quiet day at camp, time to "reflect" on everything we'd done so far. I think it was pretty much a giant time-out for me and any other mob who thought they could sneak out during the day or break Mr. Carl's rules.

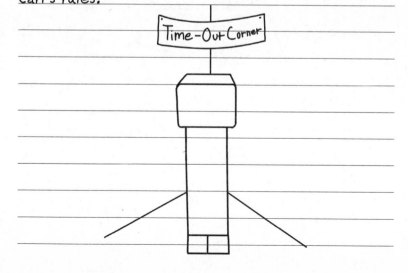

But Ms. Wanda kept saying that it was good for us to "take a pause," to spend a day sipping hot cocoa and writing letters home about all of our adventures.

There were only two problems with that plan. First of all, the cocoa wasn't hot. It was this lukewarm watered-down stuff that wasn't at ALL like the super-deluxe hot cocoa that Sam and I order at the Creeper Café back home.

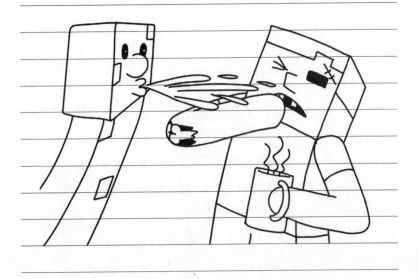

In fact, Ms. Wanda's hot cocoa wasn't even as good as the stuff we get in the vending machine at school.

How can a witch who brews POTIONS manage to botch a whole batch of hot cocoa?

The other problem with Ms. Wanda's plan is that NO mob writes letters anymore. I mean, why would we? We have our mothers VIDEO-CHATTING us and SNAPGHASTING us and HUMILIATING us all over social media. Letters, schmetters. Mom probably doesn't even know what those are anymore.

So Thursday was pretty much a bust—a giant waste of a perfectly good night in the Taiga.

But after all that pausing and quiet time and "reflecting," I can't get to sleep. So I'm trying to work on my 15-day plan.

15-Day Plan for having FUN

- Don't let Chloe get inside my head. (She's not in my head, but she's still MESSING with me big-time, thanks to Mom and that phone.)

- Find out where polar bears live — and steer clear. (I don't know where they live. Which means I must be doing a good job of steering clear, right?)

- Build a snow golem that whips snowballs at Chloe until she hands over our phone. (Well, I built the golem, but... SIGH)

- Take awesome pictures of the Taiga and win the Snapghast contest!!! (So far, so good.)

Wait, I just thought of one more:

- Block Mom's posts so she can't TOTALLY humiliate me. (Must. Do. This. But how?)

So now I'm thinking about Mom and that phone. The phone has been nothing but trouble from the beginning, right? Chloe won't share it—except for the time when she flung it at me so that Mom and I could have a loud and super embarrassing video-chat. And Chloe used the phone to rat me out for going outside during the day.

106

I can't block Mom from social media—I mean, she IS my mom, after all. But maybe . . . I can block Chloe.

YES. I CAN!

So I just did. I deleted her from my "Friends" list on Snapghast, just like that. And now I'm wondering why I didn't do that a LONG time ago.

But now I have another idea: a GENIUS idea. Hold on a sec.

Okay, I'm back. I just borrowed Sam's tablet, which was NOT easy. (I had to slide it out from underneath that sleeping slime.) And I wrote a text:

"Dear Mom and Chloe. I've decided that Chloe should really keep our phone all to herself. She takes SUCH great photos with it, and besides, I'm really trying to UNPLUG out here in the Taiga. If you need to get a hold of me, send a message to Sam. Thanks for understanding. Peace out, Gerald."

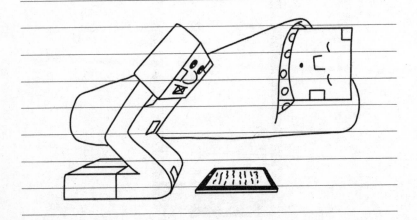

There. Done.

Now Chloe won't be flinging the phone at me to video-chat with Mom. She won't see my photos on Snapghast. And if Mom tries to reach me on Sam's tablet and I don't feel like talking, I'll just blame Sam—who isn't very good about checking his messages.

I'm feeling better already!!! So who knows? Maybe there's something to this "take a pause" thing after all.

What I learned today: Sometimes it's smart to pull out a genius plan, dust it off, and make it even BETTER.

DAY 9: SATURDAY

So there's one thing we hadn't done yet in the Taiga—at least not until last night.

SLEDDING.

I happen to be a big fan of sledding. Back home, I have this green sled that has been nothing but good to me. So when Mr. Carl said we were going to sled here in the Taiga, I figured he'd pull a batch of sleds out of the main cabin, just like Ms. Wanda did with the pumpkins.

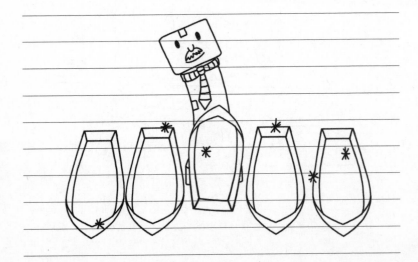

But I should really know better by now, right?

Mr. Carl isn't going to hand over ANYTHING until after he makes us learn a thing or two. So he said we were actually going to MAKE our own sleds—out of thatched tree branches and rope.

GREAT.

I mean, I've never ridden a spruce tree branch down a hill, but I'm pretty sure no mob has ever won any races that way.

Whatever. I followed the rules and grabbed a bunch of branches and tied them up with rope. But the whole time I was thinking that after we did this lame little science lesson, Mr. Carl would surprise us with a whole cabin full of REAL sleds.

But he didn't. Instead, he made us carry our homemade sleds up a SUPER steep and icy hill. There was this frozen waterfall next to the hill, which was kind of cool. But after hiking uphill for five minutes, my legs were SO heavy. And when I tried to sled down, my "sled" got stuck after moving like THREE FEET. Yup. I came to a total and complete STOP.

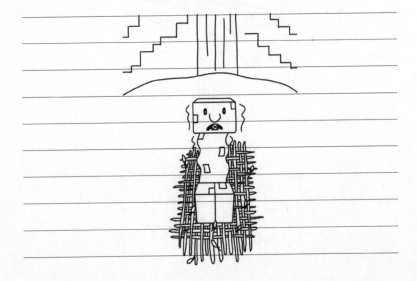

Sam whizzed by me, but I think that's because the slime was spilling out all around his sled—and slime is slippery. How do I know this? Because one time last winter, my sled was busted, and I actually rode SAM down a hill. (Turns out, he's really terrible at steering. That ride ended with a ginormous crash. But that's a whole other story.)

Some of the other mobs were having trouble, too. Willow Witch, Chloe, and Cora made one LONG sled they could all ride together. But even Willow's potion of swiftness couldn't help that sorry sled slide down the hill. I guess you can't make something go FASTER if it's not even moving at all.

Then Mr. Carl said he had an idea—a way to "use the environment" to help build a better sledding hill. HUH? Sometimes I wish that creeper would just say what he means.

Turns out, all he meant was "add water." Remember the frozen waterfall beside the sledding hill? Well, when Mr. Carl broke the ice with a pickaxe, water gushed down the hill. And you know what happens when you run water over snow and ice? It makes a WATER SLIDE.

WOO-HOO!!! I flew so fast down that slide, I felt like I was zooming in a minecart. No, FASTER than a minecart.

About halfway down, I got one of my genius ideas. I decided to borrow Sam's tablet, hike even HIGHER up the hill, and take a video of speeding down the water slide. I could post it on Snapghast instead of a photo!

Sam wasn't crazy about the idea at first. "What if you get my tablet wet?" he asked.

GOOD POINT. So I did something I never thought I'd do. I went back to the cabin and yanked one of Mom's sweaters out of my backpack.

I swore I'd never wear them, but this was a special case. I could protect Sam's tablet on the way uphill by tucking it under my super thick, super itchy wool sweater. Then I could take an award-winning video on my way down the hill. And anyway, I'd be flying along so fast on that water slide, no one would even SEE my embarrassing sweater!

Sam was A-okay with that plan. So while he was watching, I stuck the tablet safely up my sweater.

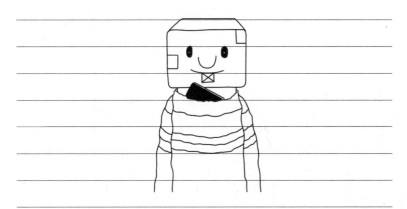

I grabbed a pickaxe from the woodpile at the bottom of the hill. And then I hiked up high on that icy hill, hoping to make the water slide even BIGGER.

I probably SHOULD have asked Mr. Carl for permission, but I couldn't find him all of a sudden. And I figured he'd say yes. I mean, my plan wasn't all about ME. I was trying to make the slide more fun for EVERY mob here. (I know—generous, right?)

Breaking the frozen waterfall was easier than I thought it would be. The ice shattered, and water poured out. I was just about to hop on my homemade sled when I spotted something—creeper footprints next to the waterfall.

Except they weren't creeper footprints. When I got closer, I saw that they were TWICE the side of my feet. And had CLAWS.

Those were POLAR BEAR tracks!!!

I'm not gonna lie—my knees got all wobbly and I almost passed out. But somehow, I managed to hop on my sled. And I flew down that water slide as if my life depended on it. I mean, it kind of DID. Those polar bear tracks were FRESH.

I was almost at the bottom when I realized I'd forgotten to take a video. CRUD!!! I grabbed the tablet to record the rest of the ride. But somehow the tablet slipped. And splashed into the water. And sailed down the slide ahead of me. NO!!!

You should have seen Sam's face when he picked up that water-soaked tablet. He wasn't the least bit worried about ME, even though I'd nearly gotten eaten by a polar bear. No, he was all about that tablet, as if it were his new best friend, gone to the great beyond WAY too soon.

Then I realized something: without Sam's tablet, I couldn't take photos. And if I couldn't take photos, I couldn't POST them on Snapghast. Which would mean I couldn't win the contest. And I'd never win a PHONE of my own!

So when Sam got all weepy, I kind of did too. After sledding, we gave his tablet a decent burial in the bottom of his backpack.

Then I did what any self-respecting creeper would do. I went to my sister's cabin and BEGGED her to let me have the phone. And she said NO. Just like that. NO.

"You told Mom you didn't want it!" said Chloe. "Why don't you just go and UNPLUG, Gerald?"

I wish my Evil Twin didn't have such a good memory. She can spit my own words back at me faster than a llama in the ~~dessert~~ desert. SHEESH.

Remind me never to tell her anything ever again. Oh, and remind me to promise Sam that I'll get a job this summer and buy him a new tablet. The poor slime can't sleep because he didn't get to have his bedtime chat with Moo. Even I'M hoping his tablet will spring back to life and show us a little cat butt onscreen.

What I learned today: Tablets + wool sweaters + water slides = DISASTER.

DAY 10: SUNDAY

So I realized something last night: we only have TWO more days in the Taiga before we load back into the minecarts and head home. Mr. Carl says we have to leave a day early, just in case we hit crummy weather in the Extreme Hills.

It HAS been cloudy lately. Every mob is complaining that they can't get reception unless they hike way uphill. Well, boo-hoo for them. I don't even HAVE a phone. Chloe won't share, no matter how much I beg her.

Now that I can't borrow Sam's tablet, I feel TOTALLY cut off from the world! I can't post photos to Snapghast. And I can't keep an eye on what Mom's posting on the field-trip blog. Who KNOWS what new ways she has come up with to totally mortify me?

This morning, I finally broke down and asked Ziggy if I could borrow his phone. It's covered in a layer of brown gunk, which I'm HOPING is just hot cocoa. He didn't have service at first, and I thought maybe that was a sign—a sign that I should avoid the germy phone at all costs. But I had my own brand-new phone riding on this. I HAD to post something on Snapghast, pronto.

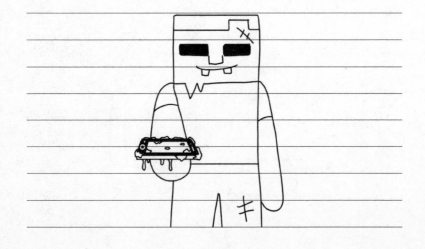

So I did. It wasn't my best work, but I figured someone should record the clouds in the sky. I mean, if you never see clouds, how can you appreciate a full moon on a clear night? And if you never have to touch a sticky, gross phone, how can you appreciate the super-clean, new one that your sister is SUPPOSED to be sharing with you?

Right after I posted the pic, I made a promise to myself. When I wake up tonight, I'm going to get that phone from Chloe—even if I have to break into her cabin and STEAL it.

What I learned today: Who CARES??? I'm tired of learning. It's time to DO something! Time is running out!!!

DAY 11: MONDAY MORNING

I will never, ever, EVER fall in love. Why? Because it turns your brain to mush.

I TRIED to get Sam to help me sneak into Chloe and Willow's cabin to get the phone. It was during dinner last night, when I KNEW Chloe wouldn't have the phone with her. For one, she doesn't have reception, now that it's so cloudy. And for two, even if she DID have a signal, she wouldn't chance a random video-chat call from Mom in the middle of the dining hall.

So I figured if Sam stood watch outside the cabin, I could sneak in and get the phone. Easy-schmeasy. But you know what he said? He said he didn't want to BETRAY Willow.

Well what's Willow got to do with anything?! Besides, I think BEST friends should come before GIRL friends, especially out here in the Taiga when you really gotta have your buddy's back. (Even Mr. Carl says so.)

Anyway, I told Sam to go enjoy his "romantic" dinner with Willow—that I would be just FINE on my own, thank you very much.

Then I snuck into the cabin and started searching. There weren't THAT many places to look: On Chloe's bed (the super messy one). On the dresser. IN the dresser. I tried to find her backpack, but it wasn't there. Then I realized she'd probably left it in the igloo on the hill, where at least she had a chance at getting a signal.

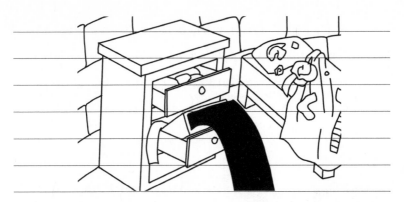

So I crept up that hill to take a look. My stomach was growling, but I told it to quiet down. I was on a mission—Operation Find That Phone.

I thought the front door to the igloo would be locked. I was even prepared to blow it up if I had to, and I'm not really a blowing-up kind of creeper. But when I pushed it, it swung open!

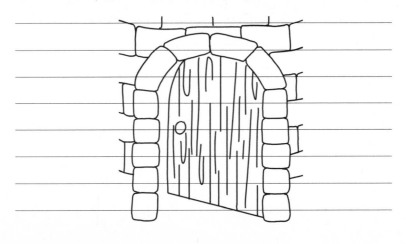

I was starting to think maybe my luck had turned around. I was SURE I was going to find the phone at any second. But I searched that frozen room from top to bottom. It. Was. Not. There.

I turned to go, but just as I was creeping out, Cora Creeper was coming IN.

"What gives, creep?" she asked.

I thought fast. I'm kind of a genius that way. "Mr. Carl said a polar bear was spotted on the hill!" I said in my most dramatic voice. "I came up here to make sure you'd locked your door. And, you know what? You didn't. Tsk, tsk. Don't you know how DANGEROUS those bears can be?"

Cora's eyes narrowed. "We DID lock our door," she said. "We always do so no one steals—"

She shut right up and glanced at the carpet in the corner of the room.

HUH. How interesting.

I used to be an undercover reporter for the Mob Middle School newspaper, and I was pretty good at it, too. So I can tell when someone is lying—or when they're scared.

So what was Cora scared of? Someone stealing a carpet? NO ONE would care about a dumb old carpet. Unless . . .

. . . there was something UNDER that carpet. Something valuable.

Now I can't sleep because I keep wondering what's under there. Did the girls dig a hole for a treasure chest? Is THAT where Chloe keeps the phone so I can't get at it? Does Willow store all of her potions in there so she can CHEAT at things like building igloos and snow golems?

I have to KNOW. And I have to find that phone. Tonight is our LAST night in the Taiga, so whoever leaves the Taiga with the phone tomorrow gets to have it all the way home. And I NEED it if I'm going to win that contest.

Plus, I can't wait to see the look on Chloe's face when she finds out I discovered her secret stash. HA!!!

That'll be an award-winning photo FOR SURE.

What I learned today: Don't judge a carpet too quickly. You NEVER KNOW what's hiding underneath . . .

DAY 11: MONDAY NIGHT

Okay, I'll admit it—I broke ALL kinds of rules today when I was SUPPOSED to be sleeping.

Broken Rule #1: I went outside during the day.

Broken Rule #2: I went WITHOUT a buddy. (GASP)

Broken Rule #3: I didn't learn A SINGLE THING.

I mean, I TRIED to learn what was hidden under the carpet in Chloe's igloo. But the door was locked. And when I started to pick the lock with my super-sneaky detective skills (and a sharp stick), a light went on inside. Turns out, the girls were sleeping in their igloo.

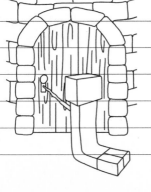

OF COURSE *they were.* Why sleep in a crummy cabin when you can snooze in an ice mansion on a hill?

I almost got busted. Willow flung the door open, and let me tell you—you do NOT want to surprise a witch with a bottle of potion in her hand.

Luckily, I was hiding behind a tree by then. I made myself real skinny so she wouldn't see me. And I thanked my lucky gunpowder that I had NOT brought my buddy with me. Because there is NO WAY Sam Slime could hide behind a tree and get away with it.

Now, after a sleepless day, I'm working on Plan B.
The "B" stands for "Better luck next time, creep."
Because by tomorrow morning, our minecarts will
be leaving the Taiga, and I'll be out of chances.
No phone. No Snapghast photos. No FUN for Gerald
Creeper Jr.

I've got one more night to pull this off. Wish me
luck.

DAY 12: TUESDAY MORNING

ACK!!!

Remember how I said I didn't learn anything yesterday? Well let's just say I made up for it TONIGHT. I learned a lot. A whole lot.

For starters, when it's your last night in the Taiga and your chaperone, Mr. Carl, builds a campfire, you should probably just ENJOY it. You know, pull up a log, drink your watery hot chocolate, and sing "The Wheels on the Minecart Go Round and Round" with the rest of the poor fools sitting next to you.

Here's what you should NOT do: You should NOT creep up the hill to your sister's igloo, pick the lock, and let yourself inside. You should NOT lift up the secret carpet to see what's underneath it. And if you happen to find a trap door, you should DEFINITELY NOT lift that door and climb down the ladder to the secret room down below.

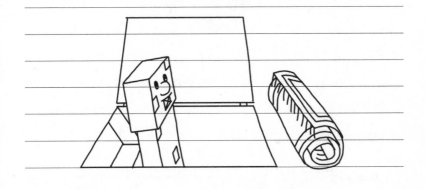

Why? Well, because that trap door is called a TRAP door for a reason. It just might TRAP you down there.

And you might not even KNOW you're trapped until you've already explored the room and found some pretty cool loot—you know, like a brewing stand, a ginormous black cauldron, a shelf filled with potion bottles, and right there on a table in the corner, a PHONE.

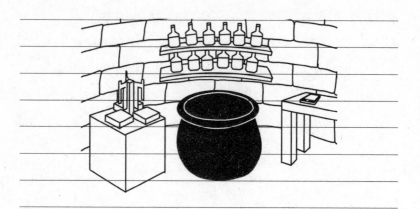

Now if you're lucky, you brought your backpack with you, so you can spend the night journaling and writing rap songs.

It's dark down here
Can barely breathe

But I have all
A creeper needs.

I've got my phone
I've got my pack

I've got some potions
In a sack.

I've got a ladder
Got a door

But still I'm stuck.
I'm getting BORED!

If you're UNlucky, you might fall asleep in that secret room (because you REALLY didn't sleep much the day before). And when you wake up, it might be MORNING already. And you might hear your Evil Twin coming down the ladder into that secret room to find her phone—the phone that YOU have hidden in your backpack.

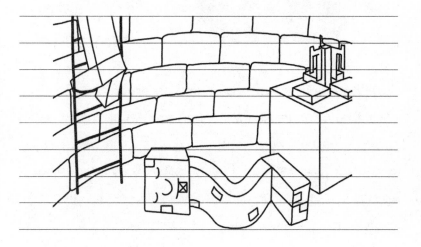

If you're a genius like me, you'll know what to do. You'll jump into that big black cauldron. But MAKE SURE you hold your breath—you know, so your sister doesn't hear you hissing, and because the cauldron will smell like fish and fermented spider eyes. GROSS.

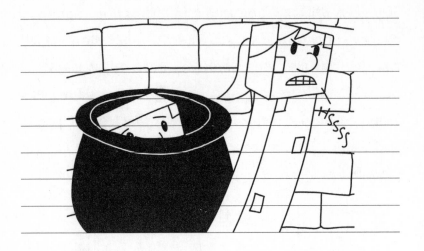

You'll hear your sister hiss on and on about how she can't find her phone. You'll hear her friends come down that ladder too and pack up every last thing they own, because the minecart is leaving soon. They'll creep back up the ladder, and you'll THINK your luck is changing—because they'll leave the pesky trap door OPEN.

But then? THEN?

Your phone might DING. Yup, you might SUDDENLY have reception in a BASEMENT while you're sitting in a big black cauldron. Go figure.

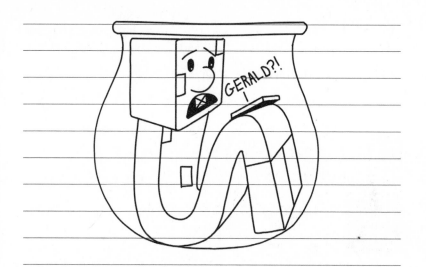

And your Mom's face will fill the screen, and she'll look really worried because you haven't talked to her for DAYS, and you'll do what NO son should ever do to his mother. You'll hang up on her.

Because, you know, you're in hiding.

And when your phone DINGs again and it's a message from your buddy Sam, asking if its okay if he rides with his girlfriend Willow for the first part of the ride home, you'll be like, FINE. I mean, that'll be the least of your worries, right?

You'll just have to sit tight for a LITTLE bit longer. Until you don't hear your sister's voice upstairs. OR until you hear the trap door slam shut.

THEN you'll leap out of the cauldron, race up the ladder, bang on the trap door, and holler for help.

SLAM!

But no mob will hear you. Because the girls have left the igloo. Everyone is running to get the

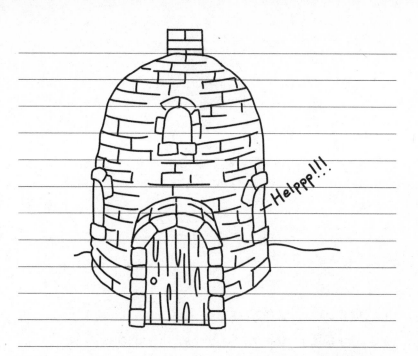

best seats in the minecarts, and NO mob is looking for you.

Because everyone thinks you're sitting with Sam.

Except for Sam, who knows you're not. And who is so ga-ga over his girlfriend that he doesn't look to see where you ARE sitting.

Which is NOWHERE.

Until you blow sky-high out of fear and desperation, and find yourself sitting in the blown-up remains of what was once an igloo castle. Way up high on a hill, where you have a perfect view of the minecarts down below.

Which are LEAVING the Taiga.

WITHOUT YOU.

DAY 12: TUESDAY MORNING (STILL)

Okay, ANY minute now, those minecarts are going to come BACK for me. Because there's NO WAY Mr. Carl will leave me to freeze out here in the Taiga, right? RIGHT???

Still waiting . . .

But I am NOT going to freak out, because I have a PHONE. And any second now, the clouds will break and I'll have reception again. Then I'll call my good buddy Sam.

Wait, I CAN'T call Sam. His tablet is broken!

So . . . I'll call Chloe. Yeah, that's what I'll do.

WAIT!!! I can't call Chloe, because I have Chloe's phone. CRUD!!!

It's okay. Deep breaths. I can call Ziggy Zombie on his crusty old phone.

I mean, I WOULD, if I had his number.

Who am I kidding??? As soon as I have a signal, I'm calling HOME. Mom will pick up. Good old Mom, who's probably worrying about me anyway. She'll know what to do. The first thing she'll do is call the principal, who will FIRE Mr. Carl. But hopefully not before Mr. Carl comes back to get me.

WHEN is Mr. Carl coming back to get me???????

If _he_ were here right now, he'd say, "What a great scientific question, Gerald! Let's test it out!"

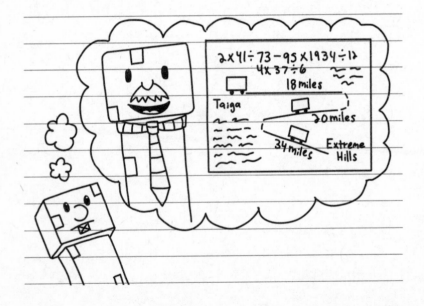

He'd have me figuring out the speed of the minecarts and the distance from here to the

Extreme Hills—and back again. We'd be drawing diagrams and sketching out minecart tracks.

But he's NOT here, Gerald. So get it together.

Oh, no. I'm talking to myself. This is NOT good!!!

It's daylight, and I'm not supposed to be out here without a buddy. This is when polar bears hunt for prey. When the wolves start howling. When the killer rabbits creep out of their dens . . .

Okay, GET A GRIP, Gerald. Snap out of it.

I just have to PRETEND that Mr. Carl and Ms. Wanda are here, and do what they would tell me to do.

First things first: Get fuel.

There are a few sticks on the ground from the torch chandelier I blew up in Chloe's igloo. That'll work. I'm going to go light them now, so DON'T go away.

Right now, trusty journal, YOU are the only buddy I've got.

DAY 12: TUESDAY AFTERNOON

Okay, a fire is blazing in the fire pit in Chloe's busted-up igloo.

I did what Mr. Carl would tell me to do. I gathered some mushrooms. Something is bubbling on the fire. It's not exactly mushroom stew, but I guess if you boil mushrooms in melted snow, it's KIND of like stew.

I'm watching for a signal on my phone, and keeping a lookout for minecarts on the tracks below. But it's

SO hard—my eyelids keep closing. This survival stuff is exhausting. And COLD.

Where's a zombie to spoon when you need one?

I did NOT just write that. Where's an ERASER when you need one???

I think I need to build a roof. That'll keep the heat in the igloo. I wish Sam were here right now—my buddy Sam, who paid attention when Mr. Carl was teaching us how to engineer the perfect roof.

But I'm going to do my best.

Pack, stack, curve. Pack, stack, curve. Wish me luck.

DAY 12: TUESDAY NIGHT

IS MR. CARL COMING BACK FOR ME?

EVER???

AM I GOING TO DIE OUT HERE IN THE COLD TAIGA???

It'll serve him right if I do. Because he never taught us what to do in THIS situation. He left a few lessons OUT of his lesson book, if you ask me.

Yeah, like you would have paid attention anyway, Gerald. You were too busy breaking rules and having FUN.

Huh? WHO SAID THAT???

Seriously, I think I'm starting to lose it up here. It's so quiet!!!

Wait, I think I hear a wolf howling. He sounds LONELY.

Dude, I know exactly how you feel. I miss my pack, too. I miss Sam's jolly jiggliness. I kind of miss Ziggy, because if he were here right now,

I'd at least hear grunts and groans instead of SILENCE. I even miss Chloe, because . . . well, no. I guess I don't really miss Chloe—not yet. But leave this creep out in the Taiga long enough, and I will.

I just tried howling like a wolf. It came out more like a long hisssssss. But I swear my voice curled around and echoed right back at me. CREEPY.

Okay, shake it off. Think positive, Gerald.

You have a roof on the igloo. It's not perfect, but it's good enough—and it has a hole in it so the smoke can get out (thanks to Sam).

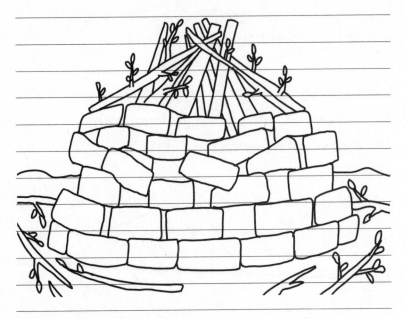

You have fuel, but these sticks aren't going to last forever.

You have a few drops of NOT very delicious, super watery mushroom stew.

Okay, what else did Mr. Carl teach you? THINK, creeper, THINK!

How fast can snow golems move? How long before they melt? What is the trajectory of snowballs off a bow and arrow?

SHEESH. NOT helpful.

I could always make a homemade sled to sleep on. Or climb way up that hill to Polar Bear Land and slide down a water slide. NOT. Or . . .

Wait, genius just struck. If there's ANY place where I might get a phone signal, it's up there— WAY up there, by the waterfall!

Genius!

But it's sure a long way up. And, I mean, I haven't slept in ages. And if I'm going to run into polar bears, I REALLY have to be well rested.

So I'm going to sleep first. And when I wake up, well . . . I guess I'm going mountain climbing.

DAY 13: WEDNESDAY MORNING

Wow, I slept the whole night away. Now it's daytime, and I'm wide awake. I really shouldn't go up the mountain during the DAYTIME, should I? All by MYSELF?

Sure, NOW you want to start following Mr. Carl's rules, Gerald.

ACK!!! It's that voice again. I CANNOT stay in this igloo talking to myself. It's time to move on. I'm going to pack up everything I have—my phone, a slimy brown mushroom, and two sticks—and head for the hills.

If I don't make it back, you'll know what happened.

Yup, I turned into Polar Bear Breakfast. I hope they're not expecting much of a meal out of me, because I'm already shrinking on this mushroom diet.

Wait, there's one thing I gotta do first.

Dear Mom,

I'm really, REALLY sorry I hung up on you today. I promise that if I make it out of the Taiga alive, I will answer EVERY time you call—even if you talk really loud and don't look at the screen and make smoochy noises and embarrass me in front of all my friends. Because that's just what moms do.

If I DON'T make it out, just remember that you've been a good mom—which I know isn't easy when you have a daughter like Chloe. Please tell her not to blame herself for my death (even if it is kind of her fault).

I hope you will all remember me the way I was:
a handsome creeper, and not the frozen green
Creep-sicle that I'm about to become.

Your smart, loyal, and faithful son,

Gerald Creeper Jr.

DAY 13: WEDNESDAY AFTERNOON

I made it to the top of the mountain. So why am I whispering? Because I'm in a CAVE.

I know, I know, it's not the smartest place for a creeper to be if he doesn't want to become polar bear food. But I STILL can't get a phone signal, and a snowstorm blew in, and I was starting to look like a snow golem out there. So what was I supposed to do???

I grabbed some spruce branches for protection. I figure I can use them like swords if I have to. And I'm going to keep my eyes open and watch for OTHER eyes—glowing eyes—in this cave. And if I need to do something to pass the time, I can always weave my branches into a sled. Or a bed.

Wait, I just had a genius idea: I can't CALL Mom, but maybe I can text her. And then the text will hang out there in cyberspace, and as SOON as there's a break in the storm, it'll PING on Mom's phone. And she'll come rescue me.

"Dear Mom. I'm in a cave at the top of a hill in the Taiga. Yup, Mr. Carl left me behind. Can you come pick me up? Just follow the frozen waterfall up the hill, and you'll find me in the first cave on the left—I mean, if I'm still here. I haven't seen any polar bears yet, but . . ."

I didn't mean to cut the message off right there, but I accidentally hit SEND. Oh, well. Mom will get the idea.

Wait, what's that noise?

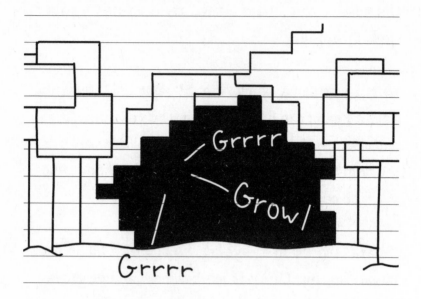

Dude, dude, dude, dude, dude . . . it was a GROWL.
Gotta go!!!!

DAY 13: WEDNESDAY NIGHT (I THINK . . .)

False alarm. The growl I heard was my own STOMACH. Mushroom stew isn't the most filling meal a creep can have.

I WISH it would stop snowing out there so I could go mushroom picking. It's wet and heavy snow, the perfect kind for snow golems.

I can't believe I'm thinking about snow golems at a time like this. But it's starting to get awfully lonely in here. Maybe if I built myself some buddies, I wouldn't go TOTALLY crazy out here in the Taiga. I could build a whole FAMILY of snow golems—I mean, if I only had a few pumpkins.

I'd even settle for a moldy old jack-o-lantern. I could name my snow golem Ziggy and pretend he was a zombie, except with better breath.

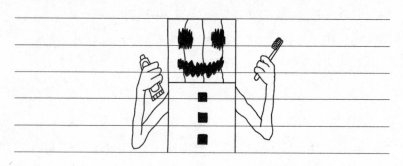

Yeah, that's what I'm going to do when it stops snowing. I'll go back down the mountain and bust my way into the main cabin. There'll be loads of pumpkins in there. And pork chops, with my name written all over them. And coal so I can make a BLAZING fire in the furnace.

Then we'll just live off the land, me and my snow golems.

Yup, that's what I'm going to do. When it stops snowing, I mean. But for now, maybe I'll just lie down on my homemade sled-bed and shut my eyes for a sec . . .

DAY 14???

Is it daytime out there? Or just the moon reflecting off the snow?

Wait, is that the light at the end of the tunnel that some mobs see when they leave the Overworld? HUH. If it is, I gotta say, it's been a good life. I can't complain much.

I mean, I would have LIKED to become a famous rapper. But maybe explorers will find my journal in this cave, and they'll give it to Mom, and she'll post all my rap songs on Instagolem and Snapghast and Hisser and Faceblock. And they'll go viral. YEAH! I

could be like that artist Van Golem who didn't really get famous until after he died.

Don't laugh. It could happen.

So I'd better get busy and do more writing. I want Mom to have PLENTY of material to work with.

Is this the end?
Dude, tell me NO

Too much to do
Before I go

Got raps to write
Got songs to sing

Got chops to eat
My FAVORITE thing...

Okay, now I'm just HUNGRY. CRUD!!!

DAY ???

I think it's thundering again out there. Is another storm rolling in? GREAT.

Wait, that's not thunder. That's . . .

A MINECART!!! Gotta go!!!

DAY 15: FRIDAY

Wow. I did NOT see all that coming. You just never know how a field trip is going to turn out.

Let me catch you up.

It was NOT thundering outside. It was definitely a bunch of minecarts, with a furnace cart blazing full of coal.

Mr. Carl really had that thing revved up. And even from way up on the mountain, I could see Sam Slime spilling out of his minecart. He wasn't sitting next to Willow anymore. Maybe he was saving a seat for me.

Maybe he was just hoping and praying that he'd see me again, his good old buddy Gerald.

"I'm here!" I shouted. "I'm here! I'm here! I'm here!"

I jumped up and down and ran in circles, but they probably couldn't hear or see me from way down below.

But you know what did?

A POLAR BEAR.

It was just a cute little thing—poking its white head up from the snow to check out this crazy creeper who was running in circles.

When I saw that bear cub, my heart melted like an igloo roof. I suddenly knew exactly why Sam wanted to meet one. I actually took a step toward it.

Until I heard growling.

UH-OH.

Yup, there was Mama Bear. And she was NOT happy to see me making friends with her cub. When she reared up on her hind legs, she was taller than an iron golem, I swear.

Now some mobs might have passed out in fear. But I am proud to say that I, Gerald Creeper Jr., did not.

Nope. I did exactly what Mr. Carl would have told me to do. I ran to the frozen waterfall and stomped on the ice to break it. When water gushed out, I

jumped on board *that* slide and FLEW down *the hill.* I
didn't even need a sled.

I *must have made it to the bottom* in record time.
And you know who was there to greet me?

MOM.

Well I've never been so happy to see that creeper
in all my life. I *might have shed a few tears*—and I
don't even care who saw me.

Mom looked kind of crazy, like she hadn't slept in days. And she looked FIERCE—like a Mama polar bear who'd just found out someone was messing with her cub.

Turns out, Mom DID get my text. And she took a high-speed minecart to the Extreme Hills, where she ordered Mr. Carl to turn his minecarts AROUND and go back to get her son.

Mr. Carl was ashamed of himself, I could tell. He hissed and stammered and apologized like a gazillion times. I should have been mad at the creeper, but

for some reason, I wasn't. Maybe it was because
I hadn't totally followed all his rules. And because
even though he'd left me in the Taiga, he'd kind of
SAVED me too—with his science lessons.

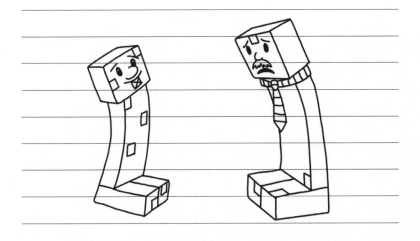

I told him about gathering fuel, about making
mushroom stew, and about the water slide. I talked
REALLY loud when I described the polar bears,
because I wanted everyone to hear me.

Sam got all weepy, like he was worried about me.
Even Chloe looked kind of impressed. "Did you get

a photo?" she asked. Leave it to Chloe to STILL be thinking about the Snapghast contest.

"Nope," I said. "I don't need one. THAT's a picture I'll never forget."

Especially the polar bear cub. I could see that cub clear as day in my head, all cute and curious about me—not scared at all. But what if I'd been a hostile mob? Or an Ender Dragon? That poor cub didn't know any better. It needed someone looking out for him.

I was like that once—like 14 days ago.

But I've grown a lot since then. From now on, I'm going to follow rules. I'm going to listen when my teacher tells me something.

Yup, you won't even recognize me. I'm going to be a whole different creeper. I mean, MOSTLY.

Chloe can spend her life posting photos if she wants to.

As for me? I'm going to LIVE my life.

But not out in the Taiga. I'm kind of done with that
for a while.

"Hey, Mom!" I said in a super loud voice, like she
did whenever she video-chatted with me. "Let's go
HOME."

DON'T MISS ANY OF GERALD CREEPER JR.'S HILARIOUS ADVENTURES!

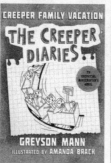

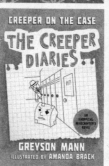

Sky Pony Press
New York